dingles&company

Odd Eggs

Warren Clone

Contents

Introduction

Eggs are extraordinary. There are so many different kinds of eggs. Eggs come in all different colors, shapes and sizes.

Eggs can be many different colors. Did you know that robins lay blue eggs? Ducks lay colored eggs, too. Some emus lay eggs that are black. Fish also lay colored eggs. Salmon lay orange eggs.

The emu lays very dark eggs which can look black, or dark blue.

Orange salmon eggs

These blue eggs are from a robin.

A toad's eggs are round.

Alligator eggs

Cylinder

Not all eggs are oval. A toad's eggs are round. The plover bird lays pear-shaped eggs. Alligator eggs are shaped like cylinders. Eggs can be many different shapes.

Odd Egg Fact
"Oval" means "egg shaped."

The animal that laid the world's biggest egg was a dinosaur. It lived long ago. The egg was as big as a basketball. (See page 11.)

Now egg sizes range from the tiny eggs of fish and insects to huge eggs from alligators and ostriches.

Odd Egg Fact
Milk snakes lay their eggs in piles of manure.

An ostrich egg

World's Biggest Birds' Eggs

An Elephant bird laid the biggest bird's egg ever found. It was a **fossilized** egg found on the island of Madagascar. This bird has been **extinct** for over 3,000 years. The egg measures 13 inches by 9 inches. It weighs over 26 pounds. It is now in a museum.

Ostrich Eggs

Ostriches lay the biggest eggs in the world. Ostrich eggs can measure up to 8 inches long and 5 inches across. They can weigh more than 2 pounds.

The shell of an ostrich egg is so tough that it can only be broken open with a hammer. The shell needs to be tough so that when the bird sits on it, the egg does not break. Ostriches are very heavy – they can weigh 300 pounds!

An ostrich looking after her eggs

Odd Egg Fact
Ducks will only lay eggs in the morning.

World's Smallest Birds' Eggs

A hummingbird sitting in her nest

A bee hummingbird egg is about the size of a pea.

The bee hummingbird is the bird which lays the smallest eggs in the world. Its eggs are less than half an inch long. They are the size of a very small pea.

You could put 4,700 bee hummingbird eggs inside one ostrich egg.

Dinosaur Eggs

Dinosaurs laid eggs. **Fossilized** dinosaur eggs were first found in the Gobi Desert in Asia. Dinosaur eggs came in many sizes.

A dinosaur with its nest may have looked like this.

Odd Egg Fact
A toad can produce as many as 6,000 eggs at a time.

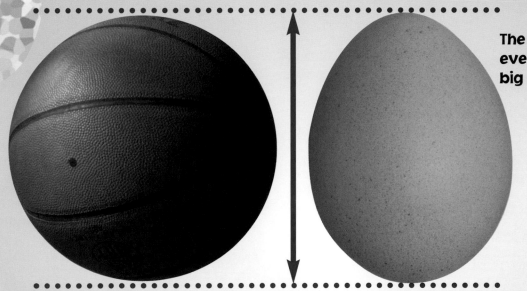

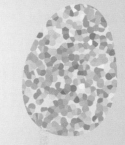

The biggest egg ever found was as big as a basketball!

The smallest dinosaur egg was only less than an inch long. A *Mussaurus* hatched from this small egg.

The biggest dinosaur egg ever found was about a foot long and over 9 inches wide. This dinosaur egg was as big as a basketball. The dinosaur egg was found in France in October 1961. The egg belonged to a dinosaur called a high ridge lizard. This type of dinosaur lived about 80 million years ago.

Expensive Eggs

Some people pay a lot of money to eat caviar.

Eggs from the sturgeon fish are called **caviar**. People sometimes have to pay a lot of money for caviar because some of these fish eggs are very rare. Caviar eggs can be black, green or brown. The rarest caviar eggs are yellow or gray. The size of the eggs varies from the size of a tiny grain to a pea.

Odd Egg Fact
The ocean sunfish lays up to 5 million eggs at one time.

Caviar can be different colors.

Designer Eggs

This Fabergé egg has another smaller egg inside it. A large, egg-shaped jewel is hidden in the center.

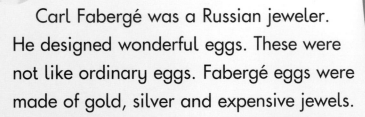

Carl Fabergé was a Russian jeweler. He designed wonderful eggs. These were not like ordinary eggs. Fabergé eggs were made of gold, silver and expensive jewels.

Each year he made a different Fabergé egg for the **Tsar** of Russia. The most valuable Fabergé egg was called the "Winter Egg." It was covered in diamonds.

Decorating Eggs

Decorating eggs can be lots of fun. It can be fun for adults as well as children. You can use hard-boiled eggs or hollow eggshells.

You can decorate your eggshells with pens and paints. Things can also be glued onto eggs — like feathers, glitter, sequins and ribbon. Funny faces and other shapes can be drawn onto eggs. Dyeing eggshells is another good way to color eggs.

You can paint or dye eggs.

Decorate hard-boiled eggs for presents.

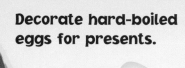

Egg decorations on a special tree

An ostrich egg decorated with sequins and ribbon

Odd Egg Fact
The world's largest omelette was made using 5,000 eggs.

How to hollow your eggs

To get a hollow eggshell, you must empty the egg. To do this, you must blow out the inside of the egg.

1. Ask an adult to make a hole in the rounded end of the egg using a needle or safety pin.
2. Ask them to make a bigger hole in the other end of the egg.
3. Place your fingers over both the holes and shake the egg.

Odd Egg Fact
The oyster can produce as many as 500 million eggs a year.

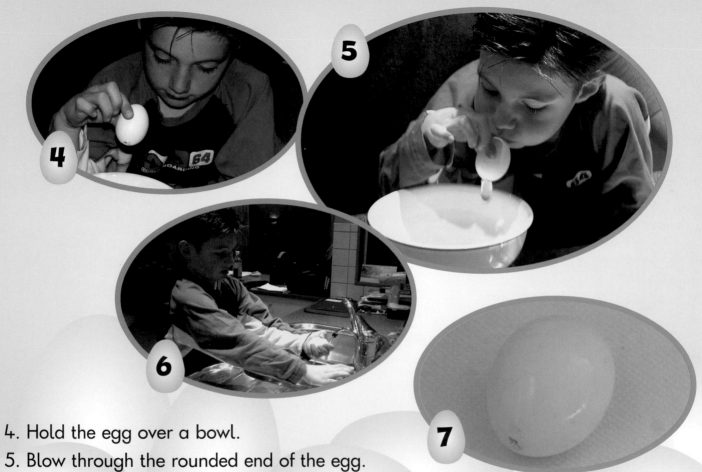

4. Hold the egg over a bowl.

5. Blow through the rounded end of the egg.

6. When the shell is empty, wash it with cool water.

7. Leave the egg to dry.

Dyeing eggs

1. Put some food coloring into a saucepan with warm water.
2. Add 2–3 teaspoons of vinegar.
3. Put the egg in the saucepan with a spoon.

4. Boil the egg in the colored water for 20 minutes, or until you like the color.

5. When the water has cooled, take the egg out of the saucepan with a spoon.

6. Leave the egg to dry.

When dyeing eggs, make sure you use an old saucepan because dye can sometimes color the inside of the pan.

Games with Eggs

Eggs are easily broken. This has made them popular for playing games.

Egg-and-spoon race

Each player is given a raw egg and a spoon. The egg is placed on the spoon. The players line up on the start line and begin the race at the same time. The winner is the first person to reach the finish line. The winner's egg must still be whole and on the spoon.

Odd Egg Fact
China produces more eggs than any other country in the world.

You are not allowed to touch the egg during an egg-and-spoon race.

20

An egg-and-spoon race is a good party game.

In London, an egg-and-spoon marathon is held each year. Dale Lyons holds the world record for this race. On April 23, 1990, Dale ran more than 26 miles. He went all this way carrying a spoon with a raw egg on it. He completed the marathon in 3 hours and 47 minutes.

Egg toss

Egg toss is another good game to play with eggs. Partners are lined up in two rows, facing each other. All the people on one side must throw a raw egg across to their partner. After each successful catch, each player steps backward to widen the gap. The pair with the last unbroken egg wins.

Odd Egg Fact
The record for the farthest egg throw is 323 feet (without the egg breaking).

A successful catch!

Glossary

caviar – These are the pickled eggs of sturgeon or other big fish. People eat these eggs as a special treat.

extinct – When something is extinct that means there are no more of its kind left alive anywhere in the world.

fossilized – The remains of an ancient animal or plant that has been preserved by being turned to stone.

Tsar – The ruler of Russia. The last Tsar died in 1917.

Index

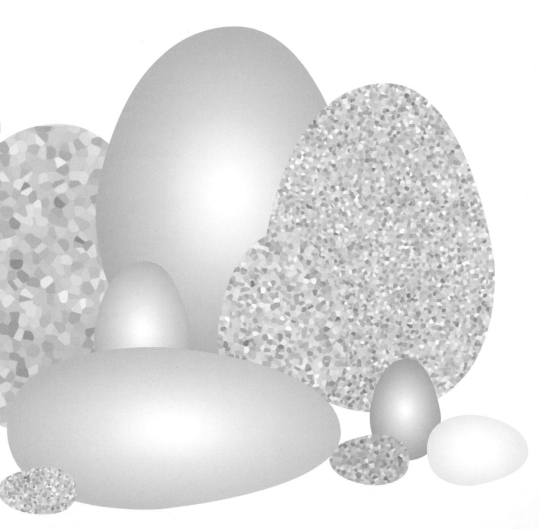